Lost

a Never novella

written by

C.S.R. Calloway

Lost: a Never novella

Copyright © 2014 C.S.R. Calloway

Published by CSRC Storytelling
Anchorage, AK 99503

ISBN-13: 978-0-9891698-5-1

Book cover designed by Shauday Smith

First Edition: April 2014

for the Philippines

and to all the world's Never children,
dreaming, lost and limitless

CONTENTS

AUTHOR'S NOTE
(#ScissorSpeaks)

I began compiling ideas for **The Neverland Novellas** last year, and among the myriad of stories I plotted and paced over, this book in particular had been initially designed as a love letter to one of my favorite childhood characters and the amazing men who had a hand in creating him. Through several unique twists of fate, it became glaringly clear to me that this story's development would have a much more unique path than my other published tales. There are times in life that God challenges us to share our gifts for unique purposes outside of ourselves.

On November 8th, 2013, Typhoon Yolanda, also known as Haiyan, left a path of death and destruction across the Philippines, worse than any other typhoon on record. ALL proceeds from this first edition book will be going forward to support two tireless organizations aiding in support and rebuilding, **The Peace Project** and **Pinoy Relief**. By purchasing this first edition book, in whatever format, you have lent a hand in restoring a piece of a home to a family that doesn't currently have one. For more information, please check out www.thepeaceproject.com/buyahouse and pinoyrelief.com. There is still lots of work to be done.

Though this novella is not dedicated specifically to them, I owe a huge debt of gratitude to AJ Rafael, Arianna Basco and Dante Basco - three phenomenal voices in every way one can have a voice - for helping lead me towards active, concentrated organizations. Thanks eternally to cover designer Shauday Smith, whose pen is mightier than Pan's sword. Thank you to my pastor, Rev. Rafer Owens of Faith Inspirational Missionary Baptist Church for being a conduit of truth and a beacon of love.

Finally, I think of my friends Dio, DJ, Josie (and Joslyn and Ryan), and Alex who formed a Sumter/Shaw AFB, South Carolina family with me, a necessary shelter from a multitude of storms. Thank you for never failing to love me for the person I am and for never failing to push me towards the person I'm striving to be. I hope, in its small way, this book honors everything you have meant to me over the years.

with an attitude of gratitude,

C.S.R. "Scissor" Calloway

Los Angeles, California
April 27, 2014

Love does not begin and end the way we seem to think it does.
Love is a battle, love is a war; love is a growing up.

- James Baldwin

COMMOTION IN THE FIRMAMENT

All children, except one, grow up, and for the rest it remains tough going. No child starts off knowing all the difficulties of growing up, which is why most babies are jolly and happy and giggle at the strange creatures called adults. Life is joy to a baby, and they find pleasure in each discovery.

There was never a fatter, happier baby than the boy who was born in Caloocan on the eve of the great Storm. As soon as he was born, his brown arms straightened towards the future and that is how his destiny was granted to him. You see, when a baby is born and reaches for his toes, he's a definite for the terrible twos and quickly develops a general obsession with money. When a baby reaches for her face, then she's doomed to live a life of everydayness. The baby who flails, unsure of up and down and surprised at the reality of being born at all is at the mercy of his or her family's wishes - turning into a ballerina who wants to be a football player or a prizefighter who wants to be a reality television star. But the baby that reaches for the future is bound to find it and master it, and this child, fat and happy, appeared ready to race to it.

As an example, he already had a full head of hair, luscious and thick and - quite unfortunately, I might add - carpeted across his forehead and down nearly to his eyelashes. No fear, the doctors assured the mother, he was not in fact a werewolf or even a bear cub, and in the coming weeks his hairline would recede back to a normal human appearance.

His mother didn't care that he was furrier than a puppy. He was her baby and she loved every portion of him. She watched him dream and she watched him eat and she watched him watch her. His happiness made her happy and she wondered what she had ever done to be happy before he had shown up.

The Storm came without warning, as storms tend to do.

Great winds had journeyed towards the city of Caloocan and the surrounding island, dancing wildly in the upper branches of the trees and whistling through the cities and hills. Excited by the winds, the dance and the whistle, the rain joined in, carefully at first, as it wasn't too sure that it could keep up with the rampaging winds.

The mother had only had the baby for a few days and they were still at the hospital when the nurses came to tell her that it was time to move, that the hospital was not safe from the winds. At first she refused, worried about what the move would do for her baby, but the winds danced harder outside, bringing down branches, ripping them from the trees as easily as one would pluck a sampaguita flower. She then understood that it was time to go. The nurses took the baby from her arms as they began to move her, and in the midst of the hurry, with people bustling everywhere throughout the hospital corridor, the power went out.

All around them outside, the wind was happily knocking down power lines and ripping trees from the ground. The rain had joined in with full force now, pouring so steadily that it was as if the entire island had been placed beneath a waterfall.

To many, it was chaos. To the winds and rain, it was an exhausting dance, and the more tired they grew, the wilder they danced, accidentally picking up bicycles, trucks, and even a baby.

It was the same furry baby, fat and happy, and the rain and winds had no idea how he had come to join the dance.

"Oh no, oh no," gravity said, reaching for the baby. "This won't do at all."

"Ours," the winds chorused, twisting and scooping wildly, keeping the baby in the dance, and the rain gave him its scent.

The winds spun the rain so tempestuously that the rain presently realized that the winds had made it quite dizzy, and it had better stop spinning so and maybe hold on to a tree or a building, at least until it got its bearings. Without the rain to dance with, the winds decided that it would be better to move on and within moments the great, terrible dance known as the Storm had ended. This left the fat, happy newborn alone, bouncing on the nothingness of air, far above the island.

Now, the baby couldn't fly, mind you, but if you don't know that you *can't* do a thing then that's the same as knowing that you *can*, so as he bounced alongside the rolling clouds, he gurgled and laughed and burped happily, and gravity did not find him.

The cloud fairies found him instead as they migrated across the sky following the rain. They saw the baby before the baby saw them, and they were so startled that a few of them forgot to flap their wings and fell at once into the vast ocean below. Cloud fairies have very heavy, sturdy wings that are able to flap through the densest of clouds, but the moment they stop their flapping, they immediately tip backwards and many of them can never right themselves up again. Because of this, many of them never stop flapping, even when they land on a sunbeam or a lost balloon. It's much too dangerous to take that chance.

The cloud fairies that hadn't fallen quickly began to orbit around the baby, forming a shimmering globe of wings and light. Other species of winged sprites, like the flower pixies or other common fairies, would have set the sky thick with fairy dust, but these fairies were still so damp from the clouds that their fairy stuff clung in gooey globs around their bodies.

How strange, they spoke in their language, tinkling and chiming. *What sky beast is this? It has no wings or strings!* But since they were all asking at once, not one of them was listening in order to answer.

A few of the fairies dove close to inspect the baby, and each time one came within a few inches of his nose, the baby giggled and squealed and the pixies would fly back into the fairy formation, frightened.

The sky beast makes music, they informed each other. *It doesn't shriek like the ones with wings that eat us and it doesn't ignore us like the ones with long tails that forget to fly.*

Each time the baby laughed, a fairy began to dance, and each time a fairy began to dance, the baby laughed. In no time, the fairies were all twirling as hard as the wind and rain had been, and their dust dried and began to sprinkle into the air.

They followed the baby as he bounced, and they danced riotously across the sky, leaving bands of purple dust, and green and orange, streaking the sky with a Great Rainbow. They began to imitate the giggles of the baby, creating harmonies that could only be beautiful to such magical creatures as fairies and babies. So loud was their merriment that they did not hear the wails arising from the Pacific islands below, of the people who had been underfoot as the winds and rain danced on top of them, and of the mother who could not find any trace of her furry, fat, happy baby boy.

MORE OR LESS AN ISLAND

Neverland starts off quite different for a lost boy than it does for its other inhabitants. You see, they are so young when they begin their journeys toward it that they aren't quite sure of what to be looking for, which means they can never actually find it. It's in that sense that they stay lost. A mad trick, really, for Neverland from that point forward remains their home and it can never be the same adventure for them as it is for the locals who are not lost and can find some excitement in the daily living, what with the whollywhomps, the pirates, and the mermaids, each more vicious than the last.

Anyway, the fortunate thing about not being able to find Neverland is that Neverland is always looking for those children who cannot find it. It's impossible to find Neverland, you see. No one does. Neverland finds you.

As you may have guessed, this baby was fated to be one of the lost boys, and one of great luck, so you shouldn't feel bad for him.

He bounced along in the sky for several days, escorted by the ferociously dancing cloud fairies and their Great Rainbow.

Seagulls flew alongside, in shock to see that the baby didn't need to flap any wings. Then one of them, the smartest it would seem, realized what the fairies had at the outset: the baby didn't even have wings. After watching the baby for a few hours, and snacking on a few inattentive cloud fairies, a few of the birds decided that he was a wingless baby bird and began feeding it. We shall leave out the details, but if you'd like a menu of what he dined on during his time in the sky, observe any local bird's feasting habits and add a side of cloud fairy purée.

In time, even the fairies tired of dancing and flying and decided to rest their wings. They dove towards the nearest spot of land, causing gravity to look up for the first time since the Storm and notice the bouncing baby.

"No, no, this won't do," gravity said again, and it began to pull the baby gently down the Great Rainbow alongside one of Neverland's many suns. "This won't do at *all*."

She found him in the upper branches of a rufilo tree, sheltered from the worst parts of the wild and protected with a bit of the pixie dust left over from the Great Rainbow. She had been traveling for several days, and had decided to take refuge from the nightly prowling creatures below.

Perspiration dotted her smooth, dark skin. It had taken her some difficulty to climb the tree, as there weren't many climbable trees in her section of Neverland, let alone any that were climbable by humans only - it was not her wish that any curious or carnivorous creatures followed her scent up the bark. Her impeccable posture - even while balanced on a rufilo branch - suggested that she had come from the north side of the Neverwood, and her dreadlocks, tied atop her head to stay free of the pack she had strapped to her back, proved that she was one of the Sandcastle peoples. Few from one side of the wood had ever traveled to the other side, as the Neverwood took up the majority of the innermost portion of Neverland and was considered the most dangerous. The woods contained the full magnitude of the glorious imaginations of all children around the world, both dreams and nightmares.

In fact, it was only the royal rulers of the Sandcastle Kingdom - all kings - who explored the depths of the Neverwood, taking yearly sabbaticals to seek a bestowal from their ancestors. This King who now joins our story had not yet received that bestowal, and she was heading back to her kingdom, the last rays of her hope fading with the last rays of the sun.

Surprised by the appearance and location of the baby, the King observed him for a few moments, then the woods, for this could very well be a trap set by the lost boys or by other inhabitants of Neverland whom she considered to be far worse than lost boys - ogres. Satisfied that this wasn't subterfuge, she allowed herself to become interested in the baby.

She crouched low, umber eyes softening, then melting as she looked at the furry, happy baby who smiled his smile of gums at her. Taking one last hardened look around, she reached for the child and he was hers and she was his.

One of her locks came loose and he grabbed it instantly, looking at her with wide eyes of wonder. He had grown some during his time in the sky, catching up with his chunkiness.

"You are not what I expected," the King said to the boy, realizing that she could never leave him, "but I cannot say I am not pleased with the ancestors for giving me you."

When the morning came, she fastened the giant leaves of the rufilo tree into a carrier so that she could strap the baby to her breast. Along with the pack on her back and the sword sheathed at her hip, she carried him down the tree, eyes roaming the leaves above and the bushes below.

Once she was comfortably on the ground she said to him, "I don't suppose you have a name. Neither do I. At least, not since I became King."

He gurgled to her, but mostly he was quiet, and she found herself talking to fill the silence that she had found so comforting just the day before.

"I have seven children," she told him when they were passing a family of wolves. "All boys. The youngest is just starting to walk. You should walk soon or he'll terrorize you."

As they found the edge of the Neverwood and the rich soil gave way to muddy dunes, she began telling him the story of her home.

"We are the descendants of Agwe and Calypso, conceived in the crescent waves under a crescent moon. Our cousins are the mermaids on the eastern shore, though long ago we chose land and earth over ocean and water. The waves still calls to us, for they remember our long-forgotten names. I suppose they always will."

They came to a simple mud hut and a man with a long braid greeted King at the door.

"Hullo, King," he said with a bow. "What have your ancestors brought to you and your people this year?"

King motioned to the baby. "Good fortune, Water's Edge."

The man ushered them into his hut. It was a small home, full of clothing and trinkets, weapons and tools, with a small spot where he slept.

"May I?" he asked once they were inside, reaching for the infant.

King gathered the baby in her arms, cooing at him before handing him over to Water's Edge.

Water's Edge held the baby away from him, staring with a sharp eye. The baby grinned gummily at him and Water's Edge traded his sharp eye for a twinkling one, cradling the baby closer.

"Well, that smile of his is contagious, that is for sure," Water's Edge said, laughing, "but I wouldn't be too sure of that good fortune." He looked up to King and his face was more serious. "He smells of rain."

King was removing the red moccasins she wore, and she didn't bother looking up. "Does he look like an ogre to you?"

Water's Edge chewed on his lip. "I've never seen a baby ogre before."

"And you've never seen a baby pigeon either," she said, placing mud-flops on her almond-shaded feet. "Doesn't mean you're holding one. I found him in the leaves of a rufilo tree, surrounded by fairy dust. Ogres are allergic to fairy dust."

"Hmm," Water's Edge said, adding nothing more.

The woman looked sidelong at the man, saying, "You are too smart to be thinking so hard." She reached for the child.

He handed the baby back, shaking his head as if clearing a fog. "I suppose."

"Thank you for the shoes, Water's Edge," King said kindly, securing the child back into the carrier. "As always, I am amazed that your nation lived so peacefully in the Neverwood, with all of the evils that make a home there."

Water's Edge chuckled. "It was relative peace. We were more peaceful compared to the pirates and the lost boys. But from the stories my mother told me, we were as wild as the wood."

"It's hard for a community to know a deep peace," King said with a small smile. "What's important is the peace within. I know that now, as a ruler and a mother."

"Wild as the wood indeed," Water's Edge agreed and they shared the laughter of adults, joys from pains.

They said goodbye in the doorway of his hut, and King moved further along the mud path, making much faster ground in her flops, being far more comfortable in them than in the moccasins.

Hundreds of Sand-dwellers began lining the road to greet their ruler and make ridiculous faces and noises at the baby, even though by this point he was sleeping away. The first several houses were made of mud, then coastal clay. The further into the kingdom they journeyed, the more the houses were decorated with shells and seaweed paste. But it didn't matter how well-to-do the neighborhood was, every single person came to the side of the road to greet King and welcome her back from her journey.

King greeted each villager with a genuine, if tired, smile. She knew the details of their family's health and status, their seabird flocks, their sandfruit crops. The journey through the kingdom was still a continuation of her sabbatical. Her connection with her people ensured that the next year would be a prosperous one, despite whatever surprises it held.

"We have to hurry home to the boys," she told the sleeping baby during the quieter moments. "They will be happy to see us."

She said this, not knowing how it would prove to be both very true and very false.

PRINCE WITH SIX ELDER

The spectacular sandcastle, visible anywhere in the kingdom of mud and clay, was a sight unlike any other in Neverland, glittering in the sunlight as blue as the morning sky. It was unlike all of the other buildings in the surrounding expanses, being made of compacted periwinkle and caramel sand from the Never shore. Its spiraling towers were giant conch shells, and clamshells provided window shade and protection from heat and wind. Atop the highest tower, lodged deep within the shingles of shingle, glimmered a tremendous blue pearl.

A ruling warrior from generations before, the grandmother of the current King, had taken the pearl from a Never dragon who wasn't too happy about it, as he had not agreed to sharing. The dragon tracked that king back to the castle and a great battle had raged. The king, victorious, wore the dragon's claws and teeth around her neck for the remainder of her reign.

The castle's throne room had been transformed by the heat of the Never dragon's flames, leaving a path of smoothed, glittering glass and ornamentations of pink, peach, purple, and brown quartz, left in the varying shapes that they had been created in and it was now known as the Quartz Hall.

The seven princes were draped haphazardly all across these quartz displays when the doors to the Quartz Hall opened. They raced towards their mother, dreadlocks bouncing across their shoulders as they reached her by order of longest legs, which was also the order of age. There were kisses and grabbing hands at her bags and carriers. The oldest handled his mother's sword with care.

"What did the ancestors bring us, maKing?" he asked, staring at the baby with a crinkled nose.

"Good fortune," she said between embraces.

"Good fortune stinks of rain," he said.

The King laughed. "And you stink of surf, maPrince. I suppose it's the duty of all boys to stink in some way, so good work. This one has just got an early start."

The older boys laughed along with their mother and reached for the baby, but the eldest stood back.

"Perhaps I'll bring a girl from the Neverwood next and she will smell like honeysuckle and sweet milk," King said, needling her oldest, but he did not respond and for several years after he said nothing more of the new addition to the castle. Not easily influenced by their eldest brother, the other princes took quickly to the young one in their initial moments with him and he was raised alongside them as an equal in blood.

The baby boy flourished under their affection and brotherly affliction. Some of the housekeepers whispered their gratitude once his forehead finally smoothed out, brown and hairless, though some of the castle's servants did note that his hair never grew long enough nor curly enough to be maintained in the style of the other princes. The older he grew, the more he brought joy to all he passed and terrorized, climbing quartz pillars and swinging from seaweed curtains and telling the most fantastic, unfinished stories before he could properly pronounce most of his words. His exuberance was contagious, most notably to King's youngest son.

The two boys were never far from each other and together they were never far from King, nestling into her arms at night, brown and silliness, arms and joy all multiplied. King and her youngest son understood the rufilo child easier than the others, perhaps because their love made their ears wiser.

The young princes kept a stash of coconuts and pineapples in a closet near the top of the grand staircase for various horseplay activities - they discovered quickly that the coconut and coral helmets of the castle guards held up well to their ammunition so they shifted their attentions to the palace gnomes with more noticeable results. King put a stop to that with a quickness.

During the day the two boys would endure tutors and swordplay lessons and elocution drills dressed royally in breezy layers of indigo and chestnut. The older boys had it worse, spending the good portion of the morning learning politics and law, while the younger ones were able to go splash in the waters an hour or so after lunch. King's sons, showing their familial connection to Agwe, were able to hold their breath for long periods of time and dive far deeper than the rufilo child could, and as he grew he began to see further differences between himself and the other princes.

One such difference was the fact that the boy had never received a name as his brothers had. Few in the Sandcastle Kingdom ever received names, and those who did - like the heirs of the royal family - had theirs changed periodically through their life according to customs.

"Six," the nameless boy asked the youngest prince on a spring afternoon as they ate lunch in the Princes' Tower, "how'd you get your name?"

Six laughed at the question, spraying bits of fish and sandfruit from his mouth. "From maKing, as is the way. We're named in the order that we come."

The nameless boy considered this. "But you're the seventh."

"Exactly!"

"Whaddya mean by 'exactly', exactly?" They were learning math, and he was quite good - good enough to know that this wasn't adding up.

"I'm the seventh," Six said, "so my name is With Six Elder."

"With Six Elder? Six elder what?"

"Six elder breddas, of course! Making me the seventh: Six."

The adopted prince looked as if he was developing a strong case of the headaches.

"So your name is Six because you're seventh?"

"Now you've got it!"

"Then, what sense does Zero's name make?"

One of the older brothers, Four, answered as he walked by, heading from one class to another. "His name is With Zero Elder."

"So because he's the first, he's Zero?" the nameless prince asked Four and Six.

"See how simple it is?" Six asked him, and he grit his teeth in response.

"Of course it becomes complicated when daughters are born," Four added, "so if the daughter has four older breddas and no older sisters, she is then With Four Elder and Zero Elder of the Other, so she would be called Four Zero-Other in case the next child was a boy so that he could be Four as both the-boy-who-would-be-Four and Four Zero-Other would have four older breddas."

The nameless boy began rubbing his temples, wondering if it would have been better to have never asked the question to begin with. Six sat across from him, happily chewing away on his fish.

"But of course if the blessed firstborn is a daughter," Four continued to explain, unaware of the affect it was having on the inquirer, "then she would just be With Zero Elder, and the first boy would be With One Elder and Zero Elder of the Other. Unless of course one of the Elders died, then everything shifts by one, or by Zero as it would be."

The nameless boy was certain he had the strongest case of the headaches ever known.

It was at this point that Zero, (the eldest, of course, if you've been following) showed his face, having listened in from the hallway.

"He doesn't need to know any of this, breddas," he said, not bothering to look at the nameless boy. "Don't waste your time; he's not royal by heritage and blood."

"What is blood where there is love?" Four asked.

"Everything," Zero responded simply. When he left, Six felt bold enough to make a face.

"Ignore him," Four whispered. "He's a soil of spoils who's just mad because he keeps growing older first, and not wiser or even bigger." Four was the biggest prince, though if Six kept eating the way he did, he might become biggest of them all.

The little one's young mind couldn't easily forget what Zero had said, nor the cold, lost feeling it gave him inside, so that night he asked King a question related to the day's conversations.

"Why don't I have a name, maKing?"

King was rubbing seaweed paste into her hair as she prepared for bed and paused in thought.

"Do you want one?"

The boy shook his head in declination. "I don't think I do. But all my breddas have names and I don't."

"Well that's according to the law," she replied. "If I had my way, all you boys would be 'Hey you, get your finger outta your nose!'"

She smiled but he didn't. "What's really bothering you, little one?"

He didn't reply. He couldn't explain how Zero made him feel like he didn't belong. How Zero made him feel like he was lost. And sometimes adults, who had forgotten the magic of youth, could not understand the otherworldly emotions of children. It was comparable to how children, without the wisdom of age, could not answer questions that hadn't been asked clearly.

"It used to be that no one could understand you because you couldn't speak well. Now you aren't understood because you choose not to speak!" King giggled for a moment, then pulled him close when she saw how upset he was. "I didn't mean to make fun, my baby of the branches. One day your mouth will grow as steady as your brain. You must remember that we are all made from the same water and earth from youngest to oldest, and that - whether we have a name or not - each of us has an important role. Otherwise we wouldn't be here, maPrince."

The boy did not say anything more, pleased that she had called him her prince. In her eyes he was still hers, and that was enough for him to feel a little less lost.

The princes were joined by a sister - Six Zero-Other, or Sixzo as they liked to call her despite the tut-tuts of palace officials - countless suns and moons later. Around this time, the two youngest boys were old enough for history sessions, and Water's Edge would make the weekly trip to the sandcastle to share his extensive knowledge of Never history and advise King on certain political matters. The boys would needle him for details about the best battles from the Sandcastle Kingdom's history, including the famed whollywhomp battle, where the fearsome beasts had woken from their hibernation and journeyed from the clouds for their waking hunt and faced down with King on her first foray into the Neverwood. They would then reenact the best parts of the battles on the castle turrets with swords they had manufactured from coconut shells and beach twigs.

Some nights, when King was away, the elder brothers (they were minus one: Zero - he would frequently travel with their mother and learn of maKing's business as he was to inherit the throne one day) would frighten the younger brothers with stories of Never dragons, brutish ogres, or lost boys. The most frightening of all was the reckless Peter Pan, a boy who never aged and never cared, bringing walking mysteries of flesh to the Neverland soil.

"Bangarang," the young boys would whisper whenever the Peter of the stories would do something awesome, chaotic, and dangerous.

"How is it that Peter and the lost boys could fly?" Six once asked his older brothers.

One responded, yawning. "There are two well known ways that boys fly. We are all born flying, you see, but growing up makes you forget. Some boys, like Peter Pan, never forgot how. The other way is with a bit of fairy dust and happy thoughts, which is what the lost boys use."

"But there is another way," Three spoke up. "Most people forget about it because it hasn't been done since before the pirates came to Neverland."

"Because it's the most dangerous way," Four interjected as One began to nod off.

Five nudged One awake, while Two asked, "Can you guess the third way a boy can fly?"

Six shook his head in declination, but the boy from the rufilo branches nodded.

"Whollywhomp fur," he said to the approving nods of the older princes. It helped having Water's Edge as a tutor. The man knew so much about beasts and Never monsters. "The fur of a whollywhomp keeps its flying capacity even if it's separated from a whollywhomp."

Two clapped the boy on the back, grinning. "That's right, breddaPrince! And what else is special about whollywhomps?"

Six knew the answer to this - he loved food as much as One loved sleep. "One serving of whollywhomp meat can keep a person free of hunger for many suns and moons. That's why the ancients kept whollywhomp jerky in storage for the kingdom, in case a sea serpent scared the fish away for a season."

"Too bad Zero's gonna be king instead of one of us," Four whispered. "He never paid attention in class like the rest of us. What would he do if the coast was ever set upon by a sea serpent?"

"Gah," Five said, "would you rather One?" The second oldest was now snoring loudly. "Our Slobber Savior, sleeping through his rule?"

Two clicked his tongue against his teeth. "It is not our place to question our King, whether she is our mother or he is our bredda. And Zero has many more years to gain wisdom from our current King." He smiled, sipping turtle wine. "She'll smack some sense into him if no one else can."

THE NIGHT OF NIGHTS

Ogres bring the rain. Usually rain arrived of its own accord across Neverland, but there were moments when it was only dragged along because of some unfortunate ogre activity. Ogres could only live where it was damp, and they had no reason to stay still just because it would keep stormy weather away from places that didn't want rain.

The Sandcastle Kingdom was such a place. With so many buildings made simply of compacted sand and mud - few so ornately constructed as the grand Sandcastle itself - rain was a huge detriment to the living situations of most sand-dwellers. Thankfully, the rainclouds rarely touched the north end of Neverland, and the air remained free of destructive wetness.

On the outskirts of the village, Water's Edge was awakened first. He made it to the door, squinting through the darkness as the splattering of water onto the sand reached his ears and helped his eyes to see what he could not believe. A mass of dark shadows in the sky reached to the very ground, clouds with arms of rain, gripping another massive shadow lumbering across the ground, trampling the neighbors' homes like puny bushes beneath the paws of a Never beast.

Water's Edge watched in silence, knowing there was no way to warn any one against a threat that should never have come. Ogres rarely ventured out of the mountains and caves, and they had never been known to travel at night.

Of course, the nameless boy didn't know any of this, so he had no reason to understand why he was so on edge the evening of the midnight rain. There hadn't been any rain in the Sandcastle Kingdom for decades, let alone since he had arrived, though there was a part of him that remembered the Storm that set him on the path to Neverland, and a deep, unreachable part of him remained unsettled whenever the clouds grew heavy over the ocean or the wind began to rustle through the lower leaves of the whispering palms.

At the sounding of the conch shell horns, King roused the two young princes in her bed.

"Watch your sister," she commanded, and swooped out of the room, blue sleeping robe rustling against the sand doorframe.

Conch shell horns meant big trouble. A sea serpent striking the crabbing boats or the Never dragon attack those generations ago. The trumpeting required immediate action from King and her warriors, even when they weren't yet sure of the specifics.

Left alone in King's bedroom, both Six and the nameless boy had racing thoughts. They were at the age children reach - and remain - where they figured they knew all the same things that adults could know, but it was in their decisions during this moment that the biggest difference between the princes shone forth.

"I'm going to see what's going on, bredda," the nameless boy announced to Six, who was clinging to the baby's crib more for his sake than for that of his sister. "Maybe I can help some."

Six could only manage a wide-eyed nod in return.

The boy stepped out into the hallway and the air was a whirl of noise and movement, arms brandishing weapons and treasures, feet running in all directions. The nameless boy stood for a moment, mentally separating the servants from the guards, finally following the watchmen who headed to the Quartz Hall below.

He dodged through the legs and fluttering robes of various palace officials and protectors, each more helpless than the last. When he reached the grand staircase overlooking the Quartz Hall he poked his head through the bannister and gasped, forgetting everything except for what he saw.

The Hall was ruined. A few of the older princes lay moaning on the shattered glass floor among some of the guards, having nobly sought to protect the castle from the invading terror. The ceiling was mostly gone, rain pounding away at the remains of the sand-constructed roof. Puddles of muddy rainwater spread across the hall, vibrating with miniature waves as the thunder echoed.

The ogre towered over all of the palace guards, gooey gray and a sickly pink, standing out from the blue powder of the now destroyed columns and the sharp remains of the busted quartz. Its face was a lumpy mash of features and its skin was the texture of coconuts. It had arrived weaponless, and it had been using a sand column as a substitute until it crushed the column into dust with its violent strength, so it picked up one of the guards and was bludgeoning the rest of the palace defenders with the poor victim.

The wild monster was lost. Ogres are known to be unintelligent creatures and this one was obviously slower than an overturned turtle.

According to the lessons that the nameless boy and Six had sat through, ogres traveled in packs and carried clubs. This one appeared to have gotten separated from its pack and had chosen to sleep someplace dry… choosing the sandcastle. Tired and bewildered - and maybe a little frightened - it hadn't chosen this war but it was not backing down.

And there was King, entering the fray with her silver sword drawn from its sheath and her eyes focused. The ogre paid her no mind, swatting down several more armored guards, so it was easy for her to get close to it and slice deeply into the monster's hide.

The ogre bellowed and swept her aside with his shrieking human weapon. She splashed into a growing puddle, soaking her robe.

"Hey, pea-brained pimpleface!" the boy yelled out, standing on top of the staircase. He held the door open to the closet where the fruit he had collected with Six sat within arm's reach.

The ogre looked at him briefly, before turning back to King, whose own eyes flicked between the beastly giant and the boy atop the stairs. Her expression was a mixture of pride and concern.

"I'm talking to you, leech-limbed slugmouth!" the boy said, tossing a well-aimed coconut and almost knocking the ogre off balance.

The ogre turned with roar and began lumbering towards the staircase, and the boy continued pelting it with pineapples and coconuts, aiming for obvious weak points, mostly in the face, causing the monster to slow.

"BANGARANG," he hollered, throwing the largest coconut he could.

The ogre caught the coconut with its teeth, crushing it open with one mighty chomp, face dripping with the milk of the fruit.

The boy was out of ammo. He stood frozen, looking down at the rampaging ogre, unsure of his next move. Suddenly he wished he had chosen to stay with Six, surrounded by the familiar walls of King's bedroom, holding to the familiar brown of his best friend. Instead he was in the middle of something too real to be a nightmare, and too familiar for him to be completely fearful, with rain dripping down his face.

If it was his time to go, he would go boldly. King had said that everyone had an important role, and maybe this was his. He was glad he didn't have too much time to dwell on it, choosing to match the ogre's roar instead. He wanted the ogre to know he was just as mighty as the monster, even if he wasn't as strong.

The ogre jerked to a halt in mid-step and its mouth flapped wordlessly. The boy stared in amazement as the ogre grabbed for the sword that had suddenly appeared in the middle of its blubbery body.

The blade belonged to King, who had discarded her muddy robe and run the beast through. She stood beneath it on the staircase in her sleeping gown, ensuring her instrument had struck true.

The ogre's potato like eyes rolled up and it collapsed backwards onto King, and together they crashed down to the glass flooring.

The rain stopped, signaling that the fight was over - the beast was dead. Several of the guards rushed over, wading through the water to move the ogre away from the King who lay silent, coated in rainwater and wet sand. The boy moved slowly along the bannister, thinking to himself that she sparkled prettier than the moonlit ocean.

The guards removed their helmets, heads bowed as the older princes struggled to their feet. Four and Five rushed in, late to the fray but swords at the ready. When they reached King, Four burst into tears and Five stood in shock.

The boy began to realize what had happened and started to rush down the stairs. Four noticed him through his tears, and met him halfway, picking him up and rushing him away from the Quartz Hall. Away from King.

King, his adopted mother, had been his home and now she was gone. It was that night that the boy, who had been growing up so steadily on the outside, first grew up a little on the inside.

WHERE THE L☠ST CHILDREN ARE

Being a lost boy starts deep on the inside. When a young soul is abandoned enough times in youth, it becomes that much more difficult for it to ever feel sheltered or loved. Being lost goes beyond just the physical, otherwise it wouldn't be so easy for Peter to take the boys who lose themselves in Neverland. But more on that will come later.

It had become immediately apparent that the nameless boy wouldn't stay in the castle in the wake of such tragedy. They had to rebuild from the destruction brought on by the ogre and the rain, and no one had time or patience for him, his swinging, his half-finished and half-understood stories, or the whispers that if he hadn't been in the Quartz Hall that night, King would still be with them.

The whispers started, of course, with Zero, who had been the first prince in the hall and the last of them to fall. He was left nursing a bandaged arm and a bruised ego, but most of all, nursing the memories of his mother.

Four took it hardest of all, thinking that he would have been a better match for the beast, though in truth, his sword skills where nowhere on par with those of his brothers. He let the nameless boy and Six share his bed, a restless sea of brown and blue, youth and anguish.

They buried King with a necklace of the ogre's teeth to honor her victory in the way of their people. One of Zero's first actions as the new King was to hang the head of the ogre from a window in the King's tower as a message to all of the Never monsters. That was followed swiftly by the nameless boy's banishment from the castle and the kingdom.

For his part, everything in the castle reminded him of King, especially her sons, as beautiful, regal and brown as she had been. His mood had drifted to something that wasn't happiness - he had never known sadness before, so he couldn't describe why he was now so discontented, but he knew something had to change. So he accepted the banishment easier than the princes did.

Six cried the morning of his departure, barely managing actual words. The nameless boy caught "bredda" "bangarang" and a seventeen syllable version of "coconut."

Two slipped him a piece of paper as the other princes joined Six in saying goodbye.

"Don't let Zero know you have this," he said, after mentioning that lazy One was still sleeping but would have been there otherwise. "This will tell you how to reach the home of one of maKing's trusted advisors. He'll be expecting you."

The nameless boy nodded and put the paper in his blue castle robe, decorated with seahorses and shells.

Three gave him a long package and made him promise not to open it until he had reached kingdom's edge.

Four gripped his shoulders, eyes wet. "What you did that night was bangarang, bredda. MaKing would have been so proud."

Five nodded, cupping the back of his head. "We're proud of you, bredda. Be well."

Six was gasping for breath and hugged the nameless boy so tight that neither of them could manage a good breath for several moments.

The guards opened the Quartz Hall doors for him, the first things repaired after the ogre attack, and once the nameless boy had passed through, he looked back to wave at the five princes who stood in the doorway watching him depart.

He stole a glance to the King's tower where Zero sat in the window next to the ogre's head, pretending not to watch.

Turning away from the sandcastle, he pulled out the paper that Two had given him and set out on the path detailed on the hand drawn map.

After a lengthy journey, where no sand-dwellers dared to acknowledge him, he reached a mudflap on the outskirts of the kingdom.

"Hullo," Water's Edge greeted him from the yard, his long braid containing more silver than when he had seen the boy last. "I thought I smelled a troublemaker."

The nameless boy stood there, overcome with too many emotions. It was nice to see a familiar face after all that had happened, but the usual greeting that Water's Edge shared with him now carried more weight.

"Is it my fault?" he asked the Indian, his face twisting in pain. "Zero always said I smelled like the rain."

Water's Edge took the boy into his arms. "No sir, it is not your fault. Rain can bring floods, or blossoms, or ogres, or rainbows." He pulled the boy from the embrace in order to look into his eyes. "Or even little princes. And then the floods, or blossoms, or ogres, or rainbows, or little princes do what they do. So blame the ogre for doing what ogres do. Do not blame the rain for what the ogre did. Or the little prince."

The boy nodded, then considered what the man had said.

"You think the rain brought me to maKing?"

Water's Edge nodded. "My nose does."

The long-haired man guided him to the entrance of his hut, saying, "Leave these cares outside. They do you no good."

As the boy entered, the man pulled a trunk from a corner of his crowded home, causing a jumble of materials to collapse into the now-abandoned space and scatter across the floor.

"Aren't you going to open it?"

His question took the boy by surprise. "The trunk?"

Water's Edge shook his head, sitting atop the trunk. "Your gift."

And the boy remembered the parcel that Two had given him. He began to rip off the covering. Inside was a sheath made from a single palm leaf and beneath it, a sword - King's sword, with the royal detailing of crescent moons and seahorses along the shaft, but seated in a coconut handle instead of the original coral handle that had shattered when the ogre collapsed down the grand staircase.

"Fitting," Water's Edge said, nodding. "And still you don't smile."

"Neither do you," the boy said, eyeing Water's Edge tiredly. "Why do you stay here in the Sandcastle Kingdom? Now that Zero's breddaKing, things will be terrible. He doesn't have any of the clear thinking that maKing had. Don't you think there might be a better place for you somewhere else in Neverland?"

"My place is with my people," Water's Edge replied, his own eyes misting over in memory, "and I have no people left here in Neverland. So you can see that the options for me are quite limited."

The boy sheathed the sword, still thinking. "That doesn't mean you have to stay. Why not go beyond Neverland?"

"You think in the limitless way of children," the older man said, opening the trunk and rifling through it, "I cannot swim, nor can I fly. Fairies rarely leave the Neverwood to come to our modest mud huts, and I don't have any happy thoughts left.

"Speaking of fairies…" He turned, arms full of clothing. "As you are not permitted to stay in the kingdom due to your older brother's impudence, I can only assume that you are going into the realm of sprites and savage beasts, two categories where fairies fit comfortably, and you must dress accordingly…"

He had the boy remove his robe and his mud-flops and began handing him different articles of clothing.

"Even though you are a Sandcastle prince, the wood has no respect of person. Wearing the royal clothes of this kingdom will do you more harm than good when you're braving the wild. It is the domain of earth, not water.”

He gave the youth red moccasins for the wood brush and red leggings and a black jacket “for the cooler weather.” The boy struggled to wrap his head around the situation at hand. Just days before he had been imagining stories of the Neverwood with Six and now he was to journey through it - no, make a home there, all on his own.

“I hope I have been a good enough teacher and you have been a good enough student to make it through those woods, my young troublemaker. Many boys in the history of Neverland have succeeded where an adult could not.”

When the boy was fully dressed, Water’s Edge handed him his coconut sword and ushered him towards the door.

“Out there, don’t lose who you are,” he said. “There is no one in Neverland like you, and you are here for a reason.”

The boy nodded, appreciating that the encouragement he was hearing was so similar to the words King had shared with him. “Thank you, Water’s Edge. Be well.”

“Be well, troublemaker.”

Leaving the hut, the boy didn’t look back. The wilderness loomed ahead and he faced it like he had faced the ogre. He reminded himself that he was just as mighty as any beast.

“Why do you sleep so much?” Six had once asked One when the older brother had fallen asleep in the middle of a diving expedition and had to be resuscitated on the shore by Two and Three. The nameless boy had witnessed the majority of this from the shore, as his diving skills were far below his poor swimming talents. He dug his feet into the silver-white beach as One peered off into the distance.

One always had a way of squinting his eyes, struggling to separate the two sides of the horizon as if he couldn’t recall which side of the line he belonged on. “I never told you?” he asked, addressing the question to both of the little princes.

“Nope,” the boy replied, jutting reed pipes along his lengthening legs, and Six shook his head in declination. They both waited as One yawned spectacularly. Two and Three had returned to the ocean to join their brothers in the hunt for food.

“I was enchanted at birth by a great sea enchantress, come ashore. Zero says that she had come to curse him and that it took her so long to reach the kingdom that I was then the freshest flesh, ripe for settling old grudges.”

“What was the curse?” the boys asked in unison.

“Oh, the old water hag couldn’t remember it properly, I think. She was an old, *old* enemy of our great-grandmaKing and her memory or her powers or both were failing with age. Instead of the typical Thousand Year Sleep or the vicious curse of Walking Death or even just cracking me open like a boiled lobster, she cursed me with eternal drowsiness." Another outstanding yawn interrupted his account. "Believe me, I would welcome the Thousand Year Sleep."

"I just thought you were lazy," the boy from the branches said truthfully and Six nodded in agreement.

"Maybe, beneath the curse, that is still true," One smiled groggily. The story and the near-drowning had taken a lot out of him. "That's why it's important to remember that there are two parts of ourselves, just as the beach has both sand and sea. The part we can't control is like the sand, put there without our permission - the hair that maKing gave you, Six, the curse that the ocean witch gave me. We can affect the other part, like the sea can be affected with currents and waves and tide." Sleep was carrying him away from them, but he was determined to finish his thought. "We can sweep the beach clean if we desire to."

"You make no sense," Six laughed.

One kept an eye open in order to respond. "Who cares for curses? I refuse to let my own troubles prevent me from helping my brothers through theirs and I refuse to let my troubles prevent me from living."

The boy spent his first night in the wood nestled alongside the sturdy leaves and branches of a rufilo tree, coat tucked close around him. It hadn't occurred to the boy to be scared, but now, in the growing darkness of the Neverwood with its strange sounds and smells, it was becoming clear to him just how fearless he would have to be.

WITH THE COMING OF PETER

The island seemed to know that Peter Pan was coming back. The birds were perhaps chirping louder as if to welcome him back into the trees. The mermaids surfaced more frequently, perhaps to catch a hint of him tagging the stars or darting between the clouds. Even the sun's beams began cutting a path through the clouds toward the deepest parts of the Neverwood, encouraging a return home for the boy who never grew up.

The boy who had once been a Sandcastle prince was adapting well to life in the Neverwood, fishing in the rivers or picking fruit from the Never trees whenever he needed a meal and running from assorted animals whenever he needed to avoid becoming a meal. At night he climbed the trees as easily as he had climbed the castle columns. The days turned into weeks and he gradually became accustomed to sleeping on branches instead of in waterbeds. The harsher adjustment was to sleeping alone.

One night, a peculiar trail of light woke him, bending through the trees and giving the faint buzz that suggested the brightness came from living creatures. He leaned carefully, trying to focus his drowsy eyes on the sight. It was brighter than the usual nighttime glimmer of the glowworms, and he made out the movement of several beings in the trail, the size of his hand and smaller. Intrigued, he grabbed his things and moved through the upper branches alongside the golden-green shimmer.

After following for several yards, the light grew almost blindingly bright. The trees themselves gave way to a giant meadow, and the boy dropped to the grass in amazement.

In the clearing were thousands upon thousands of fairies, casting a golden hue in their subdued dusting of the air. As the nameless boy took inventory based on his lessons from Water's Edge, he noticed a plethora of common fairies, from the sharp appendages of the reclusive elves to the petal-shaped wings of the socially fearless flower pixies. This was the first time he had seen a real live fairy since he had been but a baby - which of course he had no recollection of. He found himself wishing Six was here to see this.

Within moments the heavy perfume from the petal-wings had hit his nostrils and he began to smile for the first time since the night of the ogre attack. The scent of flower pixies was known to improve even the rudest of moods.

As the boy looked past the golden fairies, he noticed other boys standing around the meadow, looking as dazed and sleepy as he was, and not a single one of them older than ten. They were dressed in a range of clothing, mostly rags, but some in leaves and bark. All of them were transfixed by something at the center of the meadow.

The nameless boy knew that there had to have been other children out there in the wood - he had seen evidence of them here and there - but this was his first time seeing living boys.

He followed their gaze. What could they be looking at that he hadn't yet noticed?

Then he saw him. There, holding out his hands to the various fairies and naked as the day he was born, if he had been born at all, sat Peter Pan.

It was obvious at once that this was Peter. His eyes shown as brightly as if they were fairies themselves, and his face held a delicate balance of youth and knowledge for he had an abundance of both. His tongue sat in the corner of his mouth, gripped between his teeth as he focused on a fairy that was sprinting and tumbling across his fingertips.

"Maybe," Peter said, seeming to speak directly to the fairy. "But I haven't seen everybody yet."

The nameless boy stood in wonder. It was said that no one could speak the fairy language, but the fairy on Peter's fingers was ringing back a response.

"Who?" Peter asked loudly, growing enraged. "Where?"

He swiveled his head, taking in all of the surrounding boys.

"Hullabaloo!" Peter shouted. "Can you not see that I am naked?" He pointed to the nearest boy. "Give me your furs."

"I have no furs," said the boy, trembling. And indeed, he was dressed in an oversized shirt, using a necktie as a belt.

"Then give me what you have, No Furs," Peter commanded, and the boy obliged. Peter took the shirt, looked at the tie with disgust and gave it back.

"You can join me, No Furs," Peter announced loudly. "I'm auditioning fairies."

"For what?" another boy asked, dressed in so many clothes that the former prince wondered why Peter hadn't asked him for a few garments instead instead of the one who now only had a tie around his waist.

"For fairy duty, of course," Peter replied. "What else can do what a fairy does but a fairy?"

"Quite right, quite right," chimed in No Furs, speaking with far more authority than one wearing only a necktie had ever spoken.

"What can you do, For What?" Peter asked the boy layered in clothing. "If you're useful, you can join me as well."

"I can fish," For What replied after a pause to think terribly hard.

Peter took a few steps towards him, face twitching dangerously between glee and fury. "Do you fish for mermaids?"

For What stuttered, taken aback. "I've never seen a mermaid before in my life," he replied.

Peter's face chose glee, yet there seemed to be a bit of disappointment and the nameless boy found himself wondering if Pan had been looking for a fight. He couldn't believe how strange this boy was in person - stranger than even in the stories he had heard about him.

"You may join us, For What," Peter declared, smiling, "and I will show you a mermaid. Plenty in fact!"

Now Peter's eyes were on the nameless boy.

"Are you useful?" he asked, looking at the coconut sword sheathed at his side.

"I aided in killing an ogre!" he said proudly.

"What is an ogre?" Peter asked disinterestedly.

"I stubbed my toe," another boy said hopefully.

"Useful!" Peter said proudly, the nameless boy already forgotten. "You may join us, Eye Stubbed!"

And Peter continued on like this until every other boy there - about twelve in total - had received a name and an invitation to join him in auditioning fairies.

"Wait, what about me?" the nameless boy asked. "What's my name?"

"You don't get a name," Peter said. "I'm not keeping you."

"I'm not here to be kept," the nameless boy replied, making a face.

"Good," Peter replied quite rudely, "because I'm not keeping you. I already said so."

"That's not fair!" the boy said. "What makes me different?"

Peter stared at him for a moment, then shrugged. "That does." And he turned away.

The nameless boy stood in confusion. Peter's reply made no sense to him, and he doubted if Peter himself understood. How was this happening yet again, a group of boys excluding him for reasons that shouldn't matter? First Zero, and now…

He reacted before he could think his actions through. He didn't know how the branch ended up in his hand or how his arm decided to throw it, but suddenly the branch was clunking Peter upside his head.

Peter spun quickly, feet off the ground and fury knitting his brow.

A lopsided grin adorned the nameless boy's face, as he taunted in the style of his older brothers, "Pus pot Pan got hurt? Awww. Poor pus pot Pan." It barely fazed him that Peter was flying. Rage was working in his mind instead of wonder.

A few fairies seemed to be laughing and that made Peter far angrier. He picked up his sword from where it laid near him.

"Have at thee," Peter said, and the nameless boy drew his coconut sword.

The other boys drew back to the edge of the clearing, wide-eyed. A few of the elves looked bored and scuttled away.

"Taste my fart," the nameless boy said, leaping towards Peter and wishing he faced Zero instead. Or that ogre for a second chance.

His sword never landed, as Peter simply lifted higher into the air. Peter swung down and the nameless boy rolled into the grass, lifting his own blade. Their swords clashed and the boy on the ground kicked at the flying Pan. Peter flew back and the nameless boy bounded from the ground, brandishing his sword and his grin in cavalier fashion.

Peter stared at him for a moment, then he grinned, but his grin was different, all baby teeth. It made his face dark and terrible, and the other boy's smile fell.

Peter struck with great strength, and the force of his blow sent the coconut sword skittering across the field. Peter leveled his sword at the nameless boy's throat and even the fairies were still.

"One day your sword might move quick as your mouth," Peter said. "And that day you might be worthy of a grander defeat. But right now you're useless, so there's no point to killing you." He looked to his new crew of lost boys. "Unless one of you wants his jacket, then I'll kill him quick and we can share it!"

None of the boys were prepared for this, and none stepped forward, which is the only reason our story doesn't end here.

So Peter removed his sword from the boy's throat and walked away, having forgotten all about the fairies who, to be fair, were just as quickly forgetting about him. There would be other nights, other auditions. At this moment Peter was gathering his boys and telling them stories of mermaids and of a man he had once killed for a pair of copper-rimmed eyeglasses that he then decided he no longer wanted.

As the chatter moved further into the woods and the golden light grew dimmer, the boy simmered in anger. It was just as well, he told himself. Who wanted to be named by a jerk like Peter Pan anyway?

As he sat there in the darkening meadow, it occurred to him that maybe he had been as much of a jerk to Peter as Peter had been to him. He sighed.

He was lonely.

He picked up his sword and noticed for the first time a piece of paper secured inside of the coconut handle, shaken loose by Peter's blow.

Unfurled, the paper held a message that made the boy feel much better:

<blockquote>

Bredda,

breddaKing told us today that yu must leave the kingdum. Yu have not yet left and alreddy I miss yu and I hurt deep. I want yu to know that I am looking for ways to leave the casul and come join yu out therr in Neverland. May B I can find a ferry and I will fly to yu. Stay safe until then.

your bredda in sand and sea,

SIX, seventh prence of the sandCasul kingdum

</blockquote>

With bittersweet memories in his thoughts and Six's note clutched in his hand, the boy left the clearing with new resolve.

R⊕AR ⊕F THE BEASTS

Boys, as nature's greatest prank, never run out of ideas, they just run out of *smart* ideas. That's why, with nowhere in the wood to go, the nameless boy traveled along the coast that night, almost daring the Never beasts to track him. A generation or so ago, the coast would have been an even more dangerous place, what with pirates out and about taking the solitary boys of the island as prisoners.

That is how the nameless one came to the shores of Mermaids' Lagoon at the rise of the sun. He stripped free of his clothes and swam out to Marooners' Rock, as it was too early in the day for mermaids to be near the surface. He would have been frightened if he knew the usual danger of the mermaids, but he did not know, so instead he was glad at last to be near water that did not contain crocodiles. He was brave and bold and declared himself very loudly to be king of a rock that truly belonged to no one but the earth.

He stayed there a while, eyes closed, basking in the heat of the sun and grateful to be free of the Neverwood's canopy. Now the mermaids didn't break the surface for another reason. They sensed the coming rain.

The wind rolled the clouds onto the lagoon quickly, already dropping wetness on all below. As the clouds covered the sun and the drizzle hit the boy, he gasped and shuddered, connecting the precipitation with that fateful night at the Sandcastle Kingdom. He looked around him in the water for any sign of ogres, hugging his knees into his chest.

The rain was light and over in a few minutes as the wind swept the clouds on. The sun came out and the day began appropriately.

The boy collapsed on the stone in shock.

A rainbow streaked across the sky, painted by cloud fairies, and the mermaids finally broke the surface for the first time that day, playing with their rainbow bubbles.

They were playing the game the way a boy named John had taught them, bouncing the bubbles on their heads to keep the other mermaids from making scores, and slapping the bubbles back into the air with their tails.

The boy sat on Marooners' Rock, knees still drawn in and laughing at the bubbles. The mermaids stared closely, for, though they had seen many of his species, they had never seen one so thoroughly uninterested in them, so they did not know if they should try to drown him. Instead they watched his glee as he in turn watched the bubbles. Here is where his fortune, the same fortune sensed by the former King, protected him yet again, for if he at any point had popped a bubble, the mermaids would have certainly drowned him for his intrusion, but the wind kept the bubbles just out of reach, so the boy did not think to disturb the game, and the mermaids let him live.

The nameless boy began laughing, and the nearest cloud fairies turned to look at him. One was so startled that it forgot to flap its wings, falling in the water. This made the boy laugh again - do not think badly of him, because it didn't occur to him that this was that fairy's end - and then the cloud fairies were sure of their suspicions.

Many of them had heard this laugh before when he was a baby, and they laughed along with him in the harmonies they had learned those years ago. This made the mermaids stop as well, and then they began to imitate the fairies, and this time the sound was overwhelmingly beautiful.

The lagoon filled with the sound of musical laughter from fairies and mermaids alike, and the boy just laughed and laughed and laughed.

This changed everything for him from that day on. He realized that he could survive the rain just as easily as he could survive alongside all the various Never creatures of earth, air and sky. He realized he would be okay.

A few of the cloud fairies picked him up and carried him to shore, as they were aware of the rising tide, but even if he had decided to swim, the mermaids probably would have let him do so untroubled. The fairies tinkled and chimed to him and he told them as plainly as he could, "I have no idea what you little bugs are trying to say to me."

They dropped him back on the beach, still tinkling at him as they took back to the air. He watched them in wonder.

A few feet from him on the beach, there was a rustle in the bushes, and a young wolf burst howling onto the beach in search of the noise. The mermaids dove away at once, startling more fairies into falling and flying, but the boy did not laugh this time. He unsheathed his sword, wishing he had a bow and arrow instead.

The boy did not know it yet, but the whelp was as tame as her mother had been, and her mother was descended from a long line of tame wolves, starting with one who had been taken in by a girl visiting from outside of the island. Whenever visitors come to Neverland, they have a way of leaving their mark long after they are gone. Those that live there seem to like it the way it is and do nothing on their own to change it. Perhaps thats the nature of Neverplaces. They exist solely that outsiders may come and change it.

This whelp had gotten separated from her wolf clan, and was scrounging for food along the shores of the lagoon when she heard the celestial laughter.

The young wolf noticed the boy now, and began wagging her tale. To the boy, she seemed almost to smile. The boy cautiously returned the smile and the wolf took it as an invitation. Within moments she had bounded over towards the boy and used the momentum to knock the sword out of his hand.

As the little wolf began licking his face, the boy lay there stunned. This was the first beast from the forest that he had no need to fear or fight. He wasn't sure how to react.

The wolf scurried off of the boy and into the grass beyond the sand, barking and wagging its tail. She had tremendous energy. She brought the boy out of his melancholy the same way he had once done to King. With a smile that was beginning to feel natural, the boy grabbed his clothes and followed the wolf into the brush.

The whollywhomp wolf romp began with the wolf, actually. It may seem to you that the whollywhomp would have initiated it, but there would have been no row with a stomping whollywhomp without the romping wolf whelp.

The wolf was a new source of food provision for the boy, taking down rabbits, deer and the biggest of Never birds with ease. The boy would then skin the creatures and cook them on noon fires, or boil them into stews if he knew he was safe from Never beasts. The days rippled into weeks that flourished into months and the boy and the wolf were content, deep in the wood and far from the sandy shores of the north and the stony gulf to the east.

The forest fairies liked the wolf. They would tease her by grabbing her tail or ears and then giggle and tinkle as she would snap at them or spin in circles when she couldn't find them.

The fairies came to watch the boy, mostly, in hopes that he would laugh and create the sound they loved so much. They wouldn't reveal themselves to him usually, but he knew they were there. He had developed good senses for such things, such as noticing whenever Croc Bait was hiding behind the trees or rocks.

Croc Bait was one of Peter Pan's lost boys, the smallest one, and was an excellent sneak. The nameless boy could tell whenever Croc Bait was near, but not when he moved. Only whenever he noticed some of his food missing.

After a few weeks of sporadic visits from Croc Bait during the heavy Neverland summer, the nameless boy set a trap for him. He went fishing as he typically did, and once he had caught some fish, he set it upon a flat lemonstone and spread Never tree sap across the surface. Satisfied, he went back to the river to catch more fish, turning his back to the rock and waiting patiently for his dinner guest.

When Croc Bait appeared and hurried to sneak the fish, his hand stuck firm to the sap and he couldn't break free. He struggled in vain, panicked, even crying out as the whelp rushed towards him and danced excitedly around the rock.

"Don't dance so, Croc Bait," the nameless boy said, turning from the riverbank with more fish. "Wolves are terrible dancers." He smiled, warm and wet simultaneously. "And she knows you're not an enemy. We've seen you around, you know."

"You gonna kill me?" Croc Bait asked with wide eyes.

The nameless boy laughed. "That depends. Will you give me a reason to kill you?"

Croc Bait shook his head so quickly that the nameless boy was afraid the child would shake himself dizzy.

"Ok, then I won't kill you," the former prince said wickedly, scooping some river water up in a tree leaf. He took it to the rock, pouring it over Croc Bait's fastened hand.

Once Croc Bait's hand came free, the wolf jumped on top of him, licking him and tracking muddy paw prints across his rags of clothing.

"I guess you're hungry," the older boy said to Croc Bait. "Why didn't you just come out and ask me for food?"

"We ain't allowed ta talk to you," Croc Bait confessed. "Mosta the time."

The older boy was surprised. Why did it matter if the lost boys talked to him? "Most of the time?"

Croc Bait succeeded in getting the wolf to let him sit up and catch his breath, bird chest rising and falling with exertion and agitation. "Some-a the time Peter didn't remember you."

The nameless boy laughed. "Well, doesn't the great Pan feed you?"

Croc Bait didn't answer right off. The nameless boy no longer found it as funny as he had moments before.

When Croc Bait finally did speak, all he said was, "We're lost boys. We make do."

"What will he say if he finds out that you're here?" he asked quietly, placing the fish he had been preparing for the guest to the side and replacing it with the largest catch.

"He ain't gonna," Croc Bait replied just as quietly, but thinking other thoughts. "I only come here when he gone yonder, grabbing visitors from the outside places when he don't forget due to the winds and a fairy or two."

Croc Bait talked crazier than anyone the nameless boy had ever met. "Yonder?"

"Like Margaret, our spring cleaner," Croc Bait replied. "Not that I know what that means, but she's real nice. Brings us clothes n'things when she can. It always takes Peter a while even if he remembers her."

The nameless boy nodded as if he understood, gesturing to the fish as an invitation for Croc Bait to eat.

"I thought For What could fish," he said, watching Croc Bait devour the meal almost violently.

Croc Bait shook his head just as forcefully as he shoveled fish into his mouth, red hair dancing across his forehead. "For What lies a lot, I reckon. That was one of his lies. Peter dun beat him for it but still he does it."

"The boys who aren't as sneaky as you...how do they eat?"

Croc Bait looked up sheepishly. "What I take from you, we share back at the treehouse."

The nameless boy wanted to be mad, but he looked at the way Croc Bait's skin draped across his bones and he couldn't be. As Croc Bait started to get full, he began talking more, singing weird little songs, and playing more with the whelp.

The nameless boy watched and nearly smiled, thinking selfishly of how upset Peter would be if he saw this.

Realizing with dismay that Peter still had some hold on his thoughts, he turned in the other direction - towards the faraway lagoon - and caught his breath.

There were a few rainbows in the distance, clouds weakened from rain already blowing toward other regions of the Neverland.

He stood quickly, catching the attention of both the boy and the whelp, and the animal raced to his side, panting. He collected his things, sheathing his sword and strapping it around his waist.

"What's happening?" Croc Bait asked, wiping his face and succeeding only in spreading bits of fish and lemonstone across his face. "Where are you going?"

"I've just had an idea." The nameless boy looked into Croc Bait's eyes, eyes rippling with excitement. "I'll get you more food, and for the other lost boys, too, but you have to promise that you don't tell Peter that it's from me."

"I promise," Croc Bait said uneasily. "What are you going to do?"

The boy shook his head, implying secrets he felt no need to tell. "Meet me at Mermaid's Lagoon tomorrow around this time - just you - and I'll have something awesome ready for you," he said, rushing off into the sienna and jade of the forest, a darkening shape of crimson and coal with the wolf alongside.

The boy was appreciative of his boyhood lessons at the outset of this new escapade. He remembered that rainbows were roadways to the clouds where the whollywhomps slept, and whollywhomps could feed Croc Bait and his boy pals throughout the rest of Peter's absence, however long that may be.

He was rottenly bold, for a boy with nothing to lose has everything to gain, whether he intends to keep all of the everything or not.

It took him a few hours that felt like mere minutes due to his single-mindedness, but he and the wolf arrived at the lagoon before the last rainbow could fade. Stepping out of the leafage, he looked around carefully for predators. Seeing none, the boy started to laugh as loud as he could. In no time at all, he had gotten the attention of several cloud fairies. They danced around him, streaking the sky with their colors and strengthening the bands in the rainbow until it became a Great Rainbow.

The boy turned to the wolf. "Are you ready?"

She had no idea if she was ready or not, but when the boy stepped onto the rainbow, the wolf assuredly trotted along behind him.

The boy was sure to keep laughing, to keep the fairies dancing so that the rainbow remained strong enough to hold them up. Before long, they were high above Neverland, nearing the clouds. The laughter also kept his mood high, as the dangers of his approaching adventure could have easily left him in nervous sobs instead.

The boy took careful steps, amazed at the painted sky, the living forest, the surface of waters sparkling as if comprised of liquified fairy dust. His thoughts were purely focused on the visions bursting into his eyes as dreams made into reality. The whelp kept running to the edge of the bow, peering over and nipping at the bigger fairies who just twittered in amusement.

Eventually, the bow stretched alongside a giant cloud, full of rolling white hills. The boy signaled to the wolf and - ever so rottenly bold - took a flying leap, landing and rolling on the soft white of the cloud.

The wolf was not as keen as the boy was. She sensed the monster that was waiting for them in the sky and longed for the security of dirt and rocks.

"Come on, girl!" he said, holding out his arms and clucking gently.

She whimpered.

"I'll scratch your ear!" He glanced at the fairies now, concerned as they began moving away, knowing that the rainbow would begin losing strength sooner rather than later.

She looked at him, ensuring his promise, then vaulted clumsily over the edge of the bow, surprising them both by landing on her paws next to him on the cloud.

He laughed, scratching her behind the ear as promised. Once she was sufficiently satisfied, they raced across the cloud with abandon, kicking up cumulus clumps. It was a very large cloud, climbing higher and higher into the sky until the white very nearly merged with the blue. It was to the highest point that the boy began trekking, ruminating over long-forgotten lessons as the wolf traveled stealthily along, her senses reminding her that the cloud mountains held dangers best left to themselves.

Whollywhomps, the largest and most fearsome creatures in the greater Neverland area, have six eyes, four ears, and the snout of a bull. Their topside fur is black as night and their underfur is white as the clouds they live on, which is why many people never notice them in their lifetime. Their face, both tails, and all eight of their paws - attached to four forelimbs and four hind legs - are streaked with red.

Due to their lumbering size, they typically stay out of the Neverwood and up in the clouds, where they frequently cause coastal tornadoes if they start chasing their own tails. None of the Sandcastle princes had ever seen one themselves, but all shared the story of maKing's courageous stand against a family of them. She had not killed any, but she had sent them injured and hurrying back into the sky.

It took them longer to climb the cloud than it had taken them to climb the rainbow, and the nameless boy found himself wishing they had been able to take a nap along the way as both his mind and his limbs were growing weary, but he continued on, mindful of the shifting shapes of the cloud. He called upon all of his memories of Nevergeography and Neverhistory, grimly thinking how proud King, Water's Edge and the Sandcastle princes would be of him.

"Soon enough," the boy said mostly to himself. As if on cue, the cloud began to come apart.

The boy paused in his steps, attempting to make sense of what his eyes saw. The wolf began to growl, her senses telling her something her mind couldn't possibly know, for no Neverland creature from the ground had ever been a witness to such marvels before, and if they had, they would have known what a dangerous situation the boy and the wolf were in.

The cloud was breaking off into clumps of white about the size of the boy's head, almost like overgrown dandelion tufts bouncing gently across the shifting moisture. As they bounced closer, the boy could make out the curls of white fur and a gray, leathery seam circling across their surface.

These bouncing puffs of white were in fact baby whollywhomps (one might call them whollywimps if they were ever in fact discovered by the sorts of people who name things), and they bobbed around the boy and the wolf in an effort to discover if they were a surprise snack.

The wolf had her teeth bared, tossing her head this way and that way, daring the wimps to come closer. One did, the gray seam separating with a rush of air, revealing itself to be a mouth full of dripping fangs. At this age, all whollywimps had developed was fur, teeth and a taste for flesh, as the whollyparents were frequent with delivery of Never dragons, carnivorous sky giraffes, and the occasional flying lost boy.

The wolf attacked the wimp, avoiding its horrific mouth and grabbing it by its fur, tossing it into one of its siblings. The boy, having drawn his sword, batted a few back into the clouds. The wimps began to screech in their infant-like way, sounding like wind whistling through the leaves of the Sandcastle palms. They bounded back over towards the boy and the wolf, hard to make out against the towering white of the cloud cliff.

The boy and the wolf pup took off down the hill at full speed as the wimps gave chase, their howls digging into the boy's nerves and making him wish he had never made this journey.

Suddenly, the wimp's cries were overpowered by a thunderous bellow, and an immense whollywhomp broke through the towering wall of white behind its wimps, perhaps the tallest creature that the boy would ever see. If the boy jumped he could maybe reach one of its knees.

The whollywhomp's six eyes rolled around in their sockets until one of them found the boy, another the pup, and the rest spun between the distraught wimps. Letting out another bloodthirsty roar, the whollywhomp gave chase, and the wimps were content to let the adult do the catching.

Now fear gave the boy speed he could never have matched on his own, and he streaked across the cumulus ground in desperation.

The whollywhomp bounded over the cloud mountain behind him, its eight legs bounding, claws kicking up snow and causing the very sky to shake. It swiped at the boy with one paw as the wolf got lost in a flurry between its legs.

The boy hollered for the wolf, dodging the paw and those glinting talons. He rolled beneath the whollywhomp and dropped his sword in the chaos. He scrambled within the deep white, digging frantically to recover it.

"No, no, no, no!" he cried desperately.

The beast's two back ears turned towards him and the entire body followed suit, bounding in a wide circle.

Finding the grip of his sword, the boy pulled it free from the cloud puff, soaked to the skin in sweat and mist. Now he grinned at the incoming monster, delirious with fear and glory. This time when the whollywhomp bellowed, the boy hollered right back - "BANGARANG!" - and two of the whollywhomp's eyes widened in surprise.

The boy ran towards the beast, thrusting his sword into the first leg, spinning around the limb and rolling away as the whollywhomp stumbled.

The wolf leapt off of the surface of the cloud from wherever she had been crouching, and sunk her teeth into the whollywhomp's opposite shoulder. One of the beast's hind paws began swiping at the wolf, eyes rolling in pain, though two of its eyes remained pinned on the boy.

The boy dove for another of the giant legs, but the paw gripped him, pulling him close in a crushing grip. The boy found that struggling only restricted his movements even more. Instead he focused on moving his sword deeper into the whollywhomp. He had to be close to the beast's heart, the way its roars increased.

He was losing strength, and his breaths were growing more and more shallow. The boy drove deeper still.

He remembered the great hunts the older breddaPrinces had gone on for food excursions or rites of passage. Two had conquered the great jeweled lobster of the Seventh Fathom, while Zero had been a part of the greatest retold expedition, when two giant squid were brought back to shore and the kingdom feasted in celebration for several days. Each of the brothers had mentioned that there was a point where they thought all was lost, though they each came through in the end.

It was with this glimmer of hope that the boy slipped away into the deep unknowing of his mind, further than even sleep.

☠N THESE MAGIC SH☠RES

When the boy came to, he found himself sprawled across the white underfur of the whollywhomp, sword seated deeply in the beast. The boy sat up cautiously, realizing the giant paw that had been gripping him so tightly now lay lax out to the monster's side.

The wolf sat near him, whining pitifully.

"I say, what happened?" the boy asked the wolf.

Dear reader, what happened is this. The boy's sword indeed found the heart of the mighty whollywhomp, sending the beast belly-up quite literally. As the beast took its last breath, the fur lifted them up into the air and they drifted in the wind, safe from the whinnying wimps and comforted by the rays of the Neverland suns.

"We did it, pup," the boy said in wonderment, then set about figuring out how to best get them down from the sky.

Prince With Six Elder stood in amazement in line with his brothers, watching the horizon. The Never birds had been in a frenzy, and breddaKing had requested that Four stand watch on the turrets alongside the guards, and after a few minutes, the Prince had sent for all of his brothers as well as their sister Sixzo. Pulled from one of Water's Edge's more interesting Neverhistory lessons, Six quickly saw why Four wanted them all there.

His friend, the boy who had left the kingdom all of those months ago, was returning over the horizon, and it was a sight no one in the kingdom had ever seen, nor would likely see again in their lifetime.

The boy was flying towards the castle on a colossal carpet of red, black and white whollywhomp fur. A matching cap of fur adorned his head more like a hat than a crown, and around his neck hung a necklace of teeth and talons.

As the carpet got closer, Six noticed stacks of meat - whollywhomp meat, most likely - glistening in the sunlight and what appeared to be a tame - or at least extremely polite - wolf, also decorated with a necklace of teeth and sitting as far away from the carpet's edge as possible.

"I stopped by the hut of Water's Edge," the boy said as he floated closer, with a satisfied grin, "and was told that I might find him here."

Water's Edge stepped forward, bowing. King bristled at this display of honor. The boy bowed back as best he could while keeping balance on the fur. The whelp whined witnessing this exertion.

"Did you smell trouble?" the boy asked his former tutor with a grin.

"Over the smell of whollywhomp?" Water's Edge replied, returning the smile. "If only my nose were so conditioned."

Four was astonished. "You have brought us whollywhomp meat?"

The boy brought the carpet down, and One, Three and Five struggled uselessly with the giant, slippery body. Two, who always preferred to stay as clean as possible, called to the guards to help them.

"You've gotten big, maPrincess," he said, bowing to the young girl. Sixzo bowed in return. She was too young to remember him, but Four, Five, and Six had kept his memory alive with late night stories despite snarls from their breddaKing.

King was snarling now, but he did not speak, still trying to recover from the strangeness of the situation.

"I've also brought you this carpet, Water's Edge," the boy said, motioning to it, "with hope that you will put it to great use."

"I haven't touched whollywhomp fur since I was a tot," Water's Edge said, reaching out in wonder, fingers sinking into the bristling furs. "But why are you giving this to me?"

The boy chuckled and his courtly necklace of teeth rattled. "It's your happy thought."

Water's Edge took a sharp intake of breath. "You limitless child..."

The boy stepped off of the carpet, followed happily by the wolf, and rolled the carpet up. Three and Five tied it to the turret to prevent it from floating off.

"Have you come back to stay, Never Boy?" Six asked. King harumphed, still searching for appropriate words.

The boy shook his head. "No, Six. I'm making myself useful out in the Neverwood."

And Six noticed for the first time that even though the boy had stepped off of the carpet, he was still in the air. Grinning, the boy pointed to his red and black head covering.

"Whollywhomp fur from its paw. Who needs fairy dust?"

From behind his back he produced a duplicate of the cap, this one all white fur.

"Let's fly," he said, looking at Six expectantly. Now Six was the one catching his breath.

"I can't," Six said, stepping backwards as if the very idea of whollywhomp fur would send him careening into the sky.

The flying boy's gaze clouded. "Can't?"

Six shook his head.

"You have been trying to find me, haven't you?" the boy asked.

"What's he talking about?" King asked thinly, staring at Six.

Three snatched the white cap and thrust it in Six's face.

"Are you crazy, bredda? Go with him!"

Four and Two were cheering the idea, though One was sleeping where he stood.

Six grabbed the cap from Three, but as a source of comfort rather than possibility. "I can't do what you do," he said to the boy. "Always out there, facing down the Never beasts. Can you imagine me in front of a whollywhomp? Running belly, I should say! Even the night of the midnight rain -"

"You hush your mouth," King said. He spoke to the nameless boy for the first time. "Get out of my castle before it's your head I hang out of my window."

"breddaKing!" Two hissed, but the King's cutting gaze did not leave the boy's face.

"Technically he's not in the castle," Five snipped, and King struck him viciously in the mouth.

"Find your senses, Five," King said in a tone as sharp as his gaze. "I just aided you in the first - touch."

The boy watched this silently, then whistled to the wolf pup, which jumped into his arms. The force of the wolf's impact caused him to to flail his limbs in an effort to find balance, and his feet went wide. One of his heels connected solidly with King's chin.

"Whoa, sorry," he said, cracking a grin. "Still getting the hang of it."

He made a move to push off and his other foot found King's nose. "Gosh, sorry again, Your Majesty."

King grabbed his bleeding nose and ordered his guards to seize the boy, but the boy was already flying away and his laughter pealed through the sky.

Six stared after him, gripping the fur cap so tightly that his knuckles nearly matched it in whiteness.

"*So* bangarang," he said, voice tossed in the wind.

M☠RE USE THAN TWENTY

"Peter would like to see you."

"Peter can eat my boogers," the boy replied sleepily.

"Please don't make me go back there without you," Croc Bait said from the nearby branch where he crouched. "He'll be mighty mad."

"Then don't go back," the boy said, turning back over and pulling the rufilo branch over his shoulders.

"I can't not go back," Croc Bait hissed. "He's *Peter Pan*. He rules the winds."

"He breaks the winds," the boy snorted, then sat up to stare at the little one through a haze of stormy dreams and oceanside nightmares.

"What's the big deal? He's just a boy. You're a boy. So am I."

Croc Bait shook his head. "Peter's *different*. You know that."

The boy stared for a moment longer, then sighed. "Well you don't have to stay, but I'm sorry - I won't go with you. Peter's a jerk." He turned back over and closed his eyes.

Croc Bait poked him in the shoulder. "Peter ain't the only one who wants to see you. *She* does."

The boy sat up again. "She?"

Margaret Darling was passing out clothing to the lost boys when the nameless boy flew into the treehouse with Croc Bait.

"Hullabaloo," Peter shouted, surprised. He had been trying on one of the vinyl jackets that Margaret had brought with her and still had his arms constrained above his head.

"Bangarang," the nameless boy replied easily. He took in the lost boys who stood around, lingered on Margaret, then stared at Peter. "Are you impersonating a monkey, Pan?"

Peter twisted himself this way and that way, stopping with the jacket behind his back and giving his arms just as little freedom as before. "Of course not," he replied, rolling his eyes. "It's called *fashion*. Margaret's teaching us."

"Hi," she said, wiggling her fingers at him in a way he found strange. She tossed him a pair of black pants, ripped as if they had been in the jaws of a whollywhomp.

"Try these on," she said. Her voice was maybe weirder than Croc Bait's, who had told the boy about her. She was from the other place, one of the strangers Peter managed to bring back whenever he disappeared from Neverland for unknown days, weeks and sometimes months. The rumor was that she - and Peter's other visitors - came from the bigger lands that all of the Neverland inhabitants descended from or - in the case of the lost boys - actually traveled from.

To the boy, she looked about Five's age. Definitely older than Peter, who looked the same as he had when the boy first met him, but younger than No Furs.

"I wanted those," For What spoke up, staring at the pants and whining more than a bit. Margaret glared at him.

"Catch me a fish," she challenged him. The other lost boys laughed uproariously. She walked over to Peter, aiding him with the jacket, and he let her. Once he had it on properly, he began strutting around self-importantly.

"I'm fly and I fly," Peter was saying, more to himself than to anyone else. "I'm fly and I fly."

The nameless boy pulled the pants over his red tights.

"They look nice," Margaret said. "Do you like them? You can keep them."

He shrugged. He liked them. He wasn't sure he should show he cared.

The other boys were dressed in strange combinations of furs, silks, and the goodies Margaret had been bringing on her trips. The boy guessed that the silks had once belonged to the pirates that had destroyed the nation that Water's Edge belonged to. The same pirates that destroyed the lost boys' underground home, moving them up into the trees.

The lost boys had a phenomenal setup in their section of the woods. Whereas our hero had simply been sleeping on the branches that the trees saw fit to hold him with, the lost boys had taken some of the bendy branches of the Never trees and tied them together with tawny, pliant vines. Over the months, the branches began to naturally grow together forming floors, pathways, and bridges.

Croc Bait had called it a treehouse, but being there the unnamed boy saw that this was more of a community, high above the wood's floor where the beasts prowled. Nets of vines formed canopies, walls and storage units. Coconut halves hung throughout the vine netting and from the faint glow escaping a few of them, the boy deduced that Peter had several fairies living amongst the children. Pinecones dripped with crystalized sap that caught the luminance of fairy, moon and star, distributing it as a chandelier would in a kaleidoscope of light. Dead bark had been outfitted with the dried and stretched skin of various animals to form various modes of transportation from one "home" to the next, from gliders to sailboards.

This was beyond a simple dwelling place. This was a home. It made the boy feel sour inside. Why couldn't he have something like this? Why had maKing been taken from him so suddenly? Why did Zero hate him so?

"Croc Bait said that you wanted me," he said now, crossing his arms.

"Oh he did?"

Peter paused in his strutting and pointed to Eye Stubbed, who was chowing down on jerky. "Is he eating ogre meat?"

The nameless boy laughed. "How should I know?"

"You gave the meat to Croc Bait last week."

The boy shrugged, noticing Margaret watch him closely. "If Croc Bait got the meat from me, then it's not ogre."

"What is it, then?" Margaret asked.

"It's whollywhomp," he replied.

"I should say it is," Peter professed. "I am just surprised that *you* know what it is."

The boy narrowed his eyes. "I should know; I'm the one who killed it."

There were gasps around the camp. Margaret looked around confused.

"What is a whollywhomp?" she asked.

"The most fearsome creature in all of Neverland," For What replied.

"Tut tut," Peter said, turning towards For What. "*I* am the most fearsome creature in all of Neverland. Whollywhomps are the second most fearsome."

"Of course," For What nodded, averting his eyes, while No Furs added, "Quite right, quite right."

The nameless boy rolled his eyes. He saw Margaret crack a smile at the gesture.

"Did you request my presence just in order to ask me about whollywhomp jerky?"

"I didn't request your presence," Peter said meanly, then, after a pause, "but you can stay for a bit, if you'd like. Have some whollywhomp."

The two boys stared at each other for a moment in silence so thick only an enchanted sword could cut into it.

The boy finally spoke, knowing that Peter had won. His desire for company, however earned, overpowered his ego. "Ok. Just for a little while, though."

A little while stretched out to quite a while, as the boy fell in with their silly games, such as a hiding and seeking game where Eye Stubbed was reduced to tears because he was always found first and Peter kept making up new rules to spite him, as well as a strange game of rhythm and words that Margaret attempted to teach them about a minister's cat. Margaret finally gave up in exasperation as the boys came up with several varying adjectives to describe this cat - which was a creature that the nameless boy had never heard of before, let alone seen.

"How have you never seen a cat?" Margaret asked, amazed at this revelation which came shortly after the boy described the minister's cat as "a delicious cat."

"How have you never seen a whollywhomp?" he replied crankily, and she grinned as if this hadn't occurred to her and she was happy he had shone a light on the fact.

He noticed a few of the boys staring at him with wide eyes and open jaws. Whenever he challenged their gazes they were quick to look away, faces reddening. He didn't think he would stay much longer if they were going to be so rude and strange.

But he stayed, as Peter told half-remembered and wholly-revised stories of past adventures and Margaret told them stories of her home and strange things like playgrounds, bicycles and telephones.

Later, as all of the boys retired to their quarters, Margaret sang a soft song of a land where no one grows old. The fairies dimmed their light and even the stars were respectful of the hour, watching quietly from their positions in the sky.

"What a strange song," the boy said quietly to her when she had finished. "Is that the land you come from?"

Margaret laughed. "Not at all. Where I come from everyone grows older. Same as here." She added, "Well, except for Peter."

The boy was sitting on the edge of one of the branches, swinging his legs absentmindedly through the air. Margaret sat next to him and followed his example.

"I asked him to bring you, you know," she said. "Peter. I told him I wanted to meet you.

The boy looked at her and saw again how strange she was with her ivory skin and hair the color of coral. "Why?"

"The boys whisper of you when he's not around. I think you're as much of a legend to them as Peter is to the other people in Neverland."

"They don't like me," he said miserably.

"They are scared of you," she laughed, correcting him. "You've been surviving in the Neverwood, you have a pet wolf, and you've killed that great big sky beast that tastes like turkey."

"The wolf isn't my pet," he said. "She's my friend." He was silent for a while, before asking, "What do you know about other people in Neverland?"

She scrunched up her face in thought. "Everything there is to know, I suppose. Doesn't everyone? The Sandcastle peoples on the north shore with their castle full of boys and shore of seaweed and pearls. The beautiful mermaids and their moonlight songs of madness and longing. I've known much of it since I could think of it, really."

"That's not possible," the boy said, snorting.

She nodded with raised eyebrows. "It's very possible since it's true. Where I come from, parents and other adults always seem to think that there are things that can't happen. They say 'Never, Margaret. That would never be.' And children *know* that everything is possible, but since grown-ups are in charge of everything, we needed to hide the things they don't believe in to keep them somewhere safe. So this is where it all came. Neverland is where it's all safe. 'Never' indeed."

The boy pulled some sticky sap from the tree bark, bit half of it to chew and offered the rest to Margaret. She took it with another of her grins.

He thought of the adults he had known. maKing and Water's Edge were trustworthy enough, but when he imagined a world full of breddaKings, he shuddered. "Why do things have to be kept from grown-ups?"

"Because they ruin *everything*." To Margaret, that seemed to be the total, complete truth, but the boy wondered if there was more. He thought back on One's message of the sea and the sand, but had trouble remembering the lesson.

"Don't you think it's funny," she asked, looking off into the darkness of the branches, "that the boys here spend so much time trying to be master swordsmen and slay the most bears and lions?"

The boy remembered the battles the sand-dwelling princes had with each other, trying to come out on top in various challenges. How much it had mattered to him back then to beat Six in their swordplay.

"It's what we do?" He repeated more decisively, "It's what we do."

"I don't understand it," she said importantly, chewing on the sap. "Adults have their swords and make their wars. Kids are supposed to…play. We're not supposed to have cares." She looked at him, though her eyes were still looking into some distance. "I'm afraid I might be growing up. Why else do I feel like I don't want to be an adult, but I'm no longer a child?"

The boy wondered if all girls were this strange and thoughtful.

"I'm taking you home." The voice came from behind them, soft and sullen.

Margaret and the boy turned to see Peter sitting in the curve of a nearby branch, stained in the inkwell of the night, his eyes shining with an unnatural, intense light as he twirled his knife between his fingers.

Margaret didn't seem to be surprised or bothered by his presence. "I suppose it's that time."

"The boys are sleeping," Peter said. "You won't have to be bothered by all those silly goodbyes."

"I am ready to go," Margaret said primly, after a sigh. "My mother probably misses me dearly."

"Mothers are overrated," Peter said haughtily.

"She missed you dearly once," Margaret replied, just as haughtily. "And so did her mother." She didn't add what she was thinking inside. *And so will I - one day.* She didn't want to think about that now.

"Nonsense," Peter replied. "I don't know any mothers."

"Then how would you know that they're overrated?" Margaret said, with the same impish passion she had skewered For What with earlier in the evening.

Peter turned his glittering eyes to the boy. "You can leave now."

And for once, the boy felt no need to challenge Peter. He left easily, stepping onto the air, and gliding above the trees to let the stars and winds guide him back to his bed.

Alone once more.

HERE DREAMING, THOUGH WIDE AWAKE

Many nights later, more unwanted guests disturbed his sleep. They crashed into the tree next to him with all the elegance of flying hippopotami, causing twigs and leaves to rain down on the waking boy.

The boy sat up, gripping his sword and rubbing the sleep from his eyes.

"Well, I say," came a familiar voice. "We've reached our destination!"

"Not even! You fell asleep again!" accused a second voice, ringing just as easily on the boy's awakening ear. "I tried to steer you right but you kept going left, then you dove downward while I tried to drag you up."

The boy's mouth flopped open. "One? Six?"

The Sandcastle princes looked up in alarm, eyes growing impossibly wider when the surprise turned to recognition.

"Well, I say," One said again, and Six exclaimed, "Bredda!"

Six took an excited leap towards his friend and found no footing, instead making a swift drop through the branches.

The boy leapt from his resting place in the tree to head off Six's impending collision with the ground, swooping through the snatching branches and scanning for the familiar blue and silver robes of the palace.

To his amazement, he found Six teetering uneasily in the air, and it was only then that the boy made out the white whollywhomp cap on the prince's head.

"You're flying," he said stupidly. The wolf below - now much more wolf than whelp - took vicious leaps at the dangling heels of the prince.

Six nodded grimly, lifting his hands to steady himself. "Flying, sure. If you call it that. I can't get a decent hang of it myself." As if to provide an example, he began to lower himself to the ground, veering sharply instead into the gnarled roots of a nearby tree.

The boy flew down to steady the wolf, and One's laughter preceded his body as he descended from the upper branches to join his brothers. "You're thinking about it much too hard," he lectured Six. "Just know where you want to go and the wind will take you."

"There's no wind," Six sputtered, mouth full of leaves, dirt and grass.

"And that's why you can't fly," One said, as if this was the meaning of the universe.

"What are you two doing here?" the boy asked, before the princes could continue their increasingly hostile dialogue.

"Bredda," One said, gripping the nameless boy in a hug that wasn't entirely returned.

One had grown immensely taller, comprised it seemed of only legs, arms and dreadlocks. Six had grown in girth instead, appearing to the boy as a brown and blue blowfish, puffed to the utmost extremes and teetering through the air.

"We were looking for you," Six said, standing at a distance. "The island is abuzz with tales that you live on the clouds among the whollywhomps as their champion and king."

The boy snorted. "I am king of nothing. I am still a nameless boy of the branches."

One gazed up at the boy's sleeping place, realizing, "You sleep in the woods?"

"Where else is one supposed to sleep when he has no home?" the boy asked bitterly, cross at being awoken by the very same brothers who had let breddaKing banish him. He was especially cross with Six, who hadn't taken his invitation when the boy delivered the whollywhomp meat.

"Where did you get that hat?" he asked now, gesturing to the black fur that One wore.

"Water's Edge made us all hats from the edges of his flying carpet," One said, yawning, "even breddaKing - and boy was *he* furious." His yawn turned into a chuckle.

"He did what you said," Six said softly, "he left us a few moons ago, and he sent something for you."

Six lifted his cap, revealing a wobbly fairy, nestled in his locks and still dizzy from the flight and the recent crash.

"Water's Edge sent one to us and one to you," Six said softly. "A *messenger* fairy."

The fairy took a few unsure steps towards the edge of Six's hairline, then pulled itself up to a regal posture. Seeing the boy, the fairy bowed deep and comically before returning to its position of dignity.

The boy had never seen a fairy be so still. Noticeability equaled vulnerability in the wild. Even the boy knew how and when to hide the red of his wardrobe amongst the brown and green of the trees when a random Never beast was sensed by the whelp. This fairy, though, was clothed in pinecone scales, and quite looked like the fruit when it was motionless.

The fairy began drawing his willowy wings through his hands in a showy display. He was quite a corpulent fairy, and the boy couldn't understand how such slender wings could support its ample body. As he fluttered them, they were like living ebony strings, increasing in speed until they were just a vibrating sheen behind his body. The fairy lifted gently off of Six's head, who at once collapsed into the giggles he had been holding in as the fairy's feet had tickled him.

The boy couldn't take his eyes off of the fairy as it flew in front of Six's face and said something to him angrily. He didn't tinkle his speech like typical Never fairies, he gonged it like a miniature church bell.

Six looked up at the fairy, wiping tears from his eyes.

"I. Have. No. Idea. What. You're. Saying," he said to the fairy. One had once again fallen asleep standing up.

The fairy rolled his eyes at all of them and flew a little higher into the trees, still gonging angrily.

The wolf was curious about the fairy as well, her butt wiggling excitedly as if it was impatient for the tail to take over.

"What kind of fairy is this, again?" the boy asked Six, who replied, "Just watch."

The glittering fairy spread its arms importantly, and - this was another first vision for the boy - fairy dust burst forth from his entire being like coruscating rain from a storm cloud.

At first the dust was black, just like the fairy, but soon a stream of crimson began falling - red from the black, just as strangely and beautifully as sunsets painted purple from orange.

The red poured from his hands as if from a spout of water, falling and filling the air. As the boy watched the dust, he was amazed to see his own image, painted in the red, sullen while holding his coconut sword for the first time those months ago in Water's Edge's home. The wolf bayed.

"Say, that's a fancy trick," the boy said, surprised. He placed his hand in some of the dust, then flew higher to get a better view the fairy's presentation.

The red spun to an orange, and the boy saw Croc Bait the way he had seen him the first time, then the dust displayed a golden Margaret, from just last night.

In a swirl of green the boy saw Pan, with his peculiar innocence that was void of ignorance. The green rippled into teal, and a procession of Sandcastle princes came, leading to the deep blue reveal of maKing, gazing at him with rich compassion.

The boy had no breath to catch, and his tears fell like the dust. The fairy, effortlessly producing this rainbow of dust, was slimming down ever so slightly - so slightly in fact that at first the boy thought he was imagining it.

After maKing fell away in the shower, an ever-widening stream of undulating brown and white produced the figure of Water's Edge. Brown for his skin, and white for his hair, loose and hanging down his back.

Unlike the previous visions, this one was new to the boy's eyes, and this one spoke, the man's familiar voice filling the space between the trees and warming the night.

"Hullo." Water's Edge had a face comprised of a giant wrinkly smile. "I thought I smelled a troublemaker."

The boy smiled, and then stared at the thinning fairy in wonder. How was this possible?

"You are seeing me by way of Kadence, a messenger fairy. He is from a breed that is not found in Neverland." This was followed by a wicked smile. "I'm assuming that if you are watching this, then you have the time for one more lesson from me."

"Fairies are spawned from eggs, which is something I did not know before. They develop for quite some time within what some cultures refer to as precious stones, and they spend centuries eating their way through the jewels. Once the stone or egg is fragile enough, it cracks open, the fairy flies free, and the centuries' worth of jewel powder is excreted from their wings as what we colloquially call 'fairy dust.'"

The boy wrinkled his nose at this, looking at his shimmering hands. Fairy dust was fairy *poop*?

"Messenger fairies are distinctive in that they are 'hatched' from quite large jewels, and are noticeably, erm, *larger* than the typical fairy, though their wings are the thinnest. This is because messenger fairies are meant to fly only a few times in their life."

Here the image began a little shaky and the boy looked up in alarm at the fluttering fairy, but Kadence showed no signs of movement aside from his steadily beating wings, nor any signs of running out of dust. It was most definitely thinner, but still quite large.

Apparently the disturbance was at the source of the recording.

"Stay still, Kadence. For Calypso's sake, *stop bowing*." Water's Edge sighed. "They have a unique manners system that they seem to have captured haphazardly from certain human cultures. This has something to do with the fact that they record not only what they see when requested, they also have the ability to record what you have seen with your eyes - this they do without permission.

"This recording was most likely preceded by images Kadence captured from my eyes as well as yours. After playing it for you in full, he will then euphorically expire. Fairies, like us, must one day return to dust."

The Water's Edge in the vision brushed the ivory sparkles that were his hair.

"Something else I never would have known if it weren't for you, and this is a bit bittersweet: time passes differently outside of Neverland. There are fewer suns and moons but significantly less - or is it more? - time. The days are countable in a lifetime out here." More happy wrinkles. "I got used to it years ago, though I am terrible at explaining it. Perhaps here time is faster and shorter, but in Neverland it is slower and longer."

The Indian shrugged. "I suppose there are some things one cannot grasp in a lifetime. Take your brother Zero, who is now the sovereign King. He will never learn to trust outsiders. During his childhood, he saw what misfortune could befall a kingdom due to outsiders."

Here Water's Edge shared the history of the Sandcastle Kingdom, tales that the boy had never heard in their completeness. He learned the complete circumstances surrounding One's curse from the ancient sea witch. There was a story he had never heard about the visit from the Sun Peoples that erupted in war as they tried to sneak off with the palace gnomes. Greater still was the detailing of Four's kidnapping by the Mountain Drolls for their amusement circus (Four's nose never looked quite right after).

The tales deepened the boy's understanding of the kingdom and, most specifically, Zero's learned intolerance to outsiders, for he factored heavily in each of the story's, being the oldest brother and first in line for the throne.

"Remember to forgive your brother," Water's Edge said finally. "He may never love you as unconditionally as you love him, but it's good for you to not let the same anger and hate that drive him drive you. Remember to forgive *all* your brothers. One day they'll need your love, troublemaker. After all, sometimes trouble needs to be made. And believe it or not, one day you'll need their love in return."

The image of Water's Edge smiled, and gaps in the dust began to appear. The boy gazed at Kadence and saw that the end of the message was near. The fairy was nearly as thin as his wings.

Water's Edge spoke again. "Be well, maPrince. One final goodbye from me: Thank you for giving me enough happy thoughts to fill several more lifetimes." And with a final smile and wave, he was gone.

Kadence fluttered down gently, smiling all the way.

BETWEEN ☠NE ADVENTURE AND ANOTHER

Our current portion of the nameless boy's story comes to a jolly, peaceful end. The boy and his breddaPrinces traveled back to the lagoon to watch the mermaids surface. They journeyed without using the fairy dust, even though there was enough back in the wood to keep them flying for all eternity. They hadn't used the caps either, as Six kept spinning off through the trees and One kept requiring rest stops. So they walked instead, and the young boys slept when One slept.

Now they sat comfortably in the heat and breeze, for the shore was their habitat, bronze skin on white sand in the golden air.

They watched the mermaids swim and play and the nameless boy thought back on all he had lost. He had lost maKing and he had lost his place in the Sandcastle Kingdom. He had even lost the opportunity to join the lost boys, and there was no telling if Peter would ask him back, even if he seemed to forget he was mad just as easily as he got mad in the first place.

"Shouldn't you two be getting back before breddaKing sends the palace gnomes after you?" he asked the princes, squinting against the rising sun and scratching the wolf behind her ear.

"No, we ran away," Six said. To our hero's surprised expression, he added, "It was in protest."

One explained, "Four was kidnapped by the Mountain Drolls again. When Two asked him if he was going to go bring him back, Zero - er - King said, 'It's his own fault. He better hope that they fix his nose back.'"

The unnamed boy sat in shock. "How did it happen?"

"Well, it *was* Four's fault," Six admitted and One chuckled. "He used his whollywhomp cap to fly to their amusement park a few weeks back and heckle the exhibitions. We think he may have flown too close to the Drolls."

"You mean trolls," the boy corrected, but One shook his head.

"No, these are the Mountain *Drolls*. Trolls would offer themselves to ogres before letting themselves be so happy."

Six nodded. "So we told breddaKing that we would bring Four back ourselves."

"Good for you!" the boy of the branches said excitedly.

"Well, that was kind of a lie," Six said, elbowing One as he began nodding off. "We were kind of hoping you would join us. We didn't want to bring it up, because we were just happy to see you again. Word's been going around about the whollywhomp, and they say you may even be braver than Peter Pan."

The boy grinned. "More foolish. Definitely more foolish."

He sat there for a moment. As much as he loved the idea of rejoining his brothers, he didn't want to go back to life in the kingdom anymore. He felt like he had grown out of it. In the place of everything he had lost, he had found one adventure after another, growing in courage and knowledge, and maybe - he thought of Margaret now - maybe growing *up* a little. But just a little.

One spoke, eyes still shut, and maybe he was still asleep. "It's not a bad thing feeling like you don't belong back with us at the palace." He opened one eye, showing that he was awake. "Maybe you belong somewhere *bigger*." He closed his eyes again, spreading his arms. "Maybe this is your domain, breddaPrince."

The boy smiled, watching the seagulls chase after cloud fairies.

"Maybe," he said.

"Don't feel like you have to go with us," Six said hurriedly. "We just wanted to let you know that we'd love to have you come with us."

"Of course I'm going with you, mush-brain," the boy said, shoving Six and lifting into the air. "How else would you avoid crashing into more trees? Or worse, whollywhomps!"

Six laughed and went to join the boy, overshooting and landing among the gulls and the fairies. The brothers laughed, and fairies danced, and - well, you know how it goes from here.

After the journey to the Mountain Drolls, the boy had many more adventures, both with and without his brothers. There was his harrowing encounter with the carnivorous sky giraffes, and the time he dined with the hippopotamus emperor. There was his journey to the swampland where the ogres lived, and the time No Furs and Croc Bait dragged him into the great Neverland treasure hunt. There was his great sky duel with Peter Pan himself, and the time Peter met Sixzo and forgot all about the outside world for a time.

They are all worthy tales of honor and love, sword and spirit, and they will be shared in their time. Instead, we will end our story here, at the lagoon, amidst the flying boys and pixies, cheering, laughing, and dancing. It's important to let the happiness linger, as this story and those similar are reminders that we all knew how to fly once, and even though we grow up and forget how to, we mustn't allow ourselves to forget the way it felt.

After all, everyone of us has lost a battle or a love. Everyone of us has been lost. But the lightest heart can come after the heaviest sorrow.

Like a rainbow after the storm.

ABOUT THE AUTHOR

C.S.R. Calloway is the author of the superhero adventure *Peculiar, INC* and the upcoming *Natty Girl Saves the World*. Born in Sacramento, California, he has since been to forty-eight states and thirteen countries. He currently lives in LA, spending his time at the gym or at his keyboard, constantly redefining his bodies of work.

If you'd like for Scissor to share more stories about the nameless boy, the Sandcastle peoples, and the rest, be sure to send your thoughts to him on Facebook, Goodreads, Instagram, or Twitter.